"INSPIRED BY YOU"

CONTENTS

PART 1:
ROSCO'S LIFE & HIS RESCUE

CHAPTER 01 | THE RESCUE BEHIND THE INSPIRATION

Rosco's first day home with his new family.
(January 2016)

Hi!

My name is Rosco, and this is the story of how I found my forever home.

But before I tell you about me, let me tell you about someone very special. My sister, Roxy.

Roxy was already part of the family when I came along. Even though she was safe and loved, there was something missing in her world. She was gentle, quiet, and kind, but she often looked out the window with a soft sigh, like she was waiting for someone. She had toys and treats and a mom and a dad who adored her, but she didn't have a friend to share it all with.

Sometimes, she would bring a toy to the corner of the room and lie down with it between her paws, holding it like it was something more. She didn't bark much, and she never caused trouble. She was the kind of dog who would curl up next to you and just stay there, warm and still. However, Mom and Dad could see it: Roxy was lonely.

Mom started thinking about what Roxy might need, not another toy or a new walk route, but someone to be with her. A friend who could understand her in that special dog way. That's when Mom and Dad decided to visit the shelter in 2016.

***

Before I was Rosco, the name my mom and dad gave me, I was just another dog alone on the dusty streets. I can't remember much about my past before I was rescued by the shelter, but I do remember feeling scared, hungry, and lonely. Days turned into nights, and nights turned back into days, but nobody seemed to notice me.

Eventually, someone found me and took me to a shelter. It wasn't exactly a warm or very friendly place to be, but at least I wasn't alone anymore. I had food, a place to sleep, and other dogs nearby, even if we were all behind Kennels.

At the shelter, I waited patiently, wagging my tail every time people walked by, hoping they would see me, but they always moved on to other dogs, leaving me behind. Maybe it was because I was a Pitbull. I overheard people talk about me sometimes, saying how my breed was scary and unpredictable, but I didn't feel that I was scary. I just wanted love and care like any other dog.

After a while, I stopped hoping so much.

Then, one chilly January day, something changed. People walked around, talking softly and smiling. Suddenly, there they were. A woman and a man standing right in front of me. The woman knelt down, smiling softly. Her eyes were kind and warm, and she whispered, "Oh, look at you. You've been waiting a long time, haven't you?"

My tail started wagging faster than it ever had. I barked quietly, just a little, to let them know how happy I was.

They asked the shelter staff if we could take a walk. They were waiting for the staff to bring me outside and to them. As soon as my cage door opened, I ran in a small, excited circle, barking softly again, eager to show them that I could be a good dog. Then, I walked toward them calmly. My paws felt bouncy, my heart racing. As we walked together, the woman gently patted my fur, and her touch was so comforting. I felt safe beside them, like I had known them forever.

When we got back, I was nervous she'd leave, just like the others had. Instead, she knelt down again, stroking my ears gently. Her voice shook a little as she said, "I promise I'll be back for you in a few days. You deserve a real home, sweet boy." I tilted my head, curious about the word "home." It sounded important and wonderful. Her gentle tone made me believe her.

For the next few days, she visited me at lunchtime every day. Every time she arrived, I barked happily, running in circles inside my cage, my tail wagging so hard my whole body wiggled. Every time she left, I felt sad but also hopeful. I trusted she would return. I heard her talk to the shelter caretakers: I had to be neutered before she could take me home.

Then, finally, that special day came. I walked through the shelter doors, and when they saw me, they smiled widely. Their eyes were full of excitement. The woman clipped a leash onto my collar, and I barked joyfully, wagging my tail, hardly able to contain myself.

"Today, you're coming home with us!" she said happily, and the man with her nodded. I jumped in happy circles, feeling happier than I ever had before.

As we walked out together, I felt the warm sunlight and knew things were about to get better. We reached a place she called home. It smelled different, warm, and comforting. She knelt down, looked into my eyes, and softly explained, "This is home, Rosco. Here you are safe, loved, and you'll never be alone again."

I wagged my tail and barked softly, trying to understand and believe every word she said.

I sniffed everywhere, a bit nervous but also curious. The first few days, my new mom and dad kept me in a dog crate. They told me it was for my safety and that I would be let out once Roxy and I got used to each other.

Then, finally, I met Roxy. My new sister!

We sniffed each other cautiously at first through the cage. Roxy stood still, her ears slightly back but her eyes gentle. She didn't bark or growl. She just watched me carefully, like she was trying to figure out if I was the one she had been waiting for.

Mom gently spoke to both of us, letting us know it was safe.

Slowly, we relaxed, tails wagging gently. Soon, I was let out of the cage, and we were lying side by side, our noses touching the same blanket.

And just like that, I knew I was finally home.

CHAPTER 02 | LEARNING TO ADJUST

Mom, can you feed us? It is eating time!
(Rosco & Roxy)

It didn't take me long to realize that I loved my new home. I loved my mom and dad. I loved Roxy. I loved the soft blankets, the smells in the kitchen, and the sound of the TV at night. Yet, there was something that made me feel a little different from Roxy.

I was scared. A lot.

Even though I was safe now, sometimes my heart would beat really fast for no reason. I'd worry that Mom would leave and never come back. I worried when she picked up her keys. I worried when she put on her shoes, and when we got into the car… oh, no!!

The car made me feel terrible. My tummy would twist and turn, and I couldn't help it. Sometimes I'd get sick. It was so embarrassing.

But Mom didn't give up on me.

I think it was someday near the end of January 2016. Mom said, "Rosco, we're going to help you feel better."

She signed me up for something called "training." I didn't know what that meant at first. Soon, I found out it meant getting in the scary car (ugh) and going to a big room with other dogs and their humans. Mom told me that I was going to have one-on-one training. There were bright lights and strange smells and lots of noise. I was so nervous the first time I had an accident right there on the floor. I had pooped. I felt really bad, but Mom calmed me down.

I wanted to be good. I really did. It was just that everything felt too big and too loud and too fast. I couldn't help it. I got sick again on the way home.

Still, Mom didn't give up on me.

Every week, she took me back. She wiped up my messes. She patted my head. She told me, "Good boy, Rosco. We're learning."

Week after week, we practiced. Sitting. Staying. Walking nicely. Looking at Mom when she called my name. I didn't always get it right, but Mom always smiled and gave me treats when I tried.

Then, one day in March 2016, something amazing happened.

I graduated!

I even got a certificate. Mom took a picture of me, my tail wagging so fast it was just a blur. I didn't really understand what "graduated" meant, but I knew Mom was proud, and that made me feel like maybe… I was a little bit brave, after all.

***

But my story didn't end there.

Even though I had graduated, I was still scared of a lot of things. A broom falling, especially when Mom used it to sweep the floor. A loud truck outside. Even a sneeze sometimes made me jump.

Mom saw that I needed more help. So, in November 2016, we started another training class. This one was harder. There were even more dogs, and the exercises were tougher. Sometimes, I wanted to hide under the chair, but Mom kept bringing me, week after week, always with that same gentle voice and patient smile.

And guess what? In January 2017, I graduated again!

Another certificate! Another picture! Another waggy-tail day!

I wasn't a perfect dog. I still got nervous. I still needed Mom close by, but I was getting stronger inside, little by little.

And Roxy… oh, Roxy was the best therapy in the world.

When I got too scared, she'd nudge me with her nose or curl up next to me. She never rushed me or barked at me to be braver. She just stayed close, and that made all the difference.

However, there was one thing I couldn't seem to fix right away: my separation anxiety.

I loved Mom so much that being apart from her made me panic. When she left the house, even just for a little while, my heart raced, and I felt like the walls were closing in. I'd chew things. Anything I

8

could find. Shoes. Pillows. The corner of the couch. I didn't want to misbehave. I just didn't know how else to show that I missed her.

Mom and Dad were so patient with me. They tried all kinds of things to help. Even though it was hard, they never gave up.

One day, Mom and Dad had to leave for a big trip. Ten whole days!

They left Roxy and me with a babysitter. I could tell Mom was nervous. She kissed me on the head a thousand times before she left, whispering, "Be good, Rosco. We'll be back soon."

I wanted to be good. I really did, but it was so hard without her. I missed her so much that I chewed. And chewed. And chewed. When Mom and Dad came back, they found chewed-up chairs, couch, blanket, dog bed, and pillow stuffing everywhere.

I thought maybe they'd be mad. Maybe they'd be sorry they picked me, but when Mom walked in and saw the mess, she didn't yell. She didn't even scold me. She just knelt down, opened her arms, and let me jump into them.

"It's okay, Rosco," she said, her voice soft. "We missed you, too."

In that moment, I knew something more important than anything else: I wasn't just rescued.

I was loved, and no matter how scared I got, no matter how many mistakes I made, Mom and Dad were always going to come back.

Rosco's first training session in March 2016.

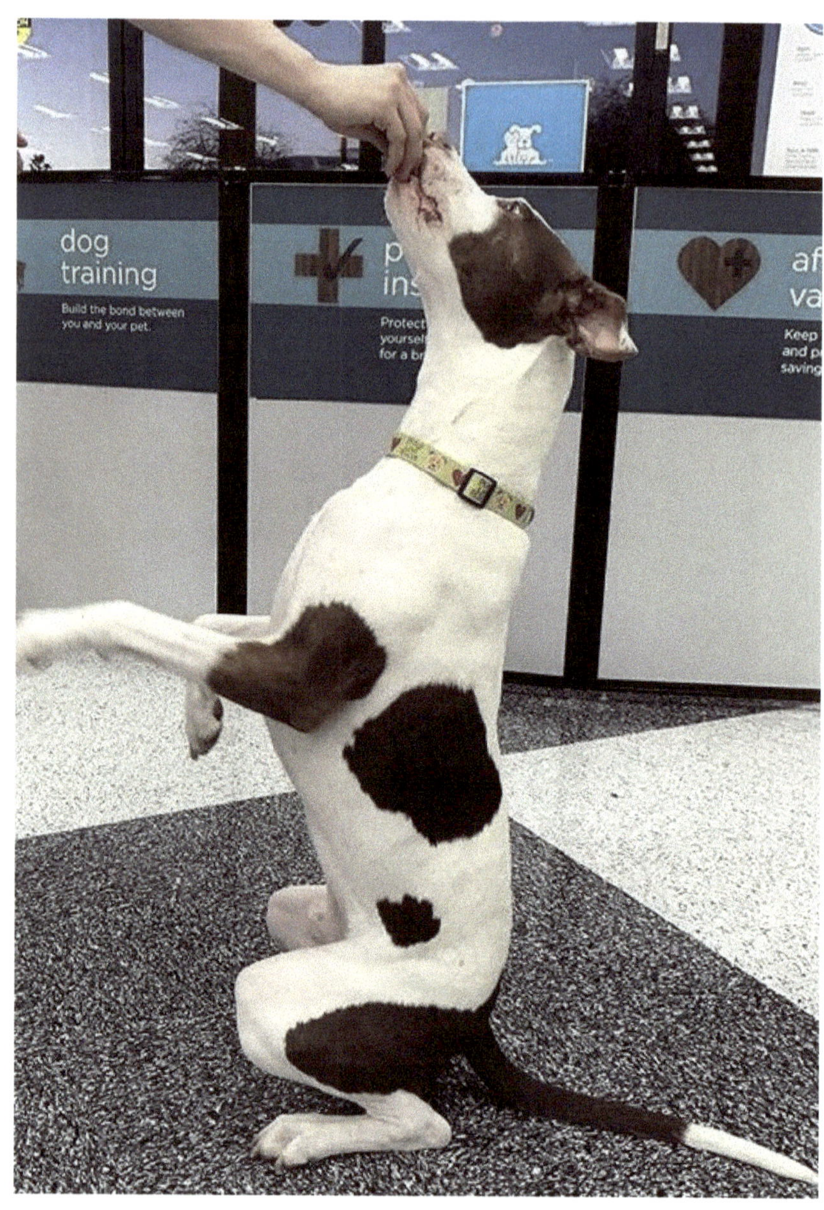

Mom & Dad left us with the babysitter.

CHAPTER 03 | LOSS OF MY SISTER ROXY

After some time, I don't know how long, but I remember that it slowly got colder outside. I liked playing outside in the sun, but winter was pretty, too. It was December 2017, and I remember that it had gotten so, so cold! The wind was sharp, but I liked it, and when I ran on the grass in the backyard, it felt crunchy under my paws.

One morning, I was running around, sniffing the corners of the fence, chasing something I thought I saw. Maybe a leaf or a bird or just a shadow? ......and then.....

Ouch!

I felt a sharp sting in my back foot.

I limped to the porch, lifting my paw and whimpering just a little. Mom came out fast when she saw me. Her face turned worried as soon as she looked down at my foot. I had never seen her look like that before.

"Oh no, Rosco," she cooed, scooping me up in her arms. "You're bleeding, baby."

The next thing I knew, we were at the vet. The smells there always made my nose twitch. They cleaned my foot, and I tried to be brave, but it hurt. Then, they gave me something called stitches. I didn't know what that meant, but I didn't like it. I just wanted to go home.

Mom held me the whole time. She kissed my head and said over and over again, "I'm so sorry, buddy. I should have been watching. I'm so, so sorry."

However, it wasn't her fault. She couldn't be everywhere at once. I wanted to tell her that.

I healed slowly, and Mom gave me extra cuddles and soft treats every day. Roxy stayed close, too. She didn't say much, but she always curled beside me when I rested.

***

The summer came.

It was August 2018.

The sun was hot outside, but our house felt quiet. I was worried because Roxy was always up to something.

Something was wrong.

I noticed that for some days, Roxy had been sleeping more. She didn't get up as fast. Her eyes were still kind, but they looked tired.

One morning, I lay beside her, like I always did. I licked her nose gently and rested my head next to hers. I knew that she wasn't feeling well, so I just wanted to be by her side and comfort her. I noticed that her breathing was slow, and it only got slower with time. I lifted

15

my head up to look at her and whimpered. I could no longer feel her breathing. I nudged her and barked softly, but nothing.

She didn't get up.

She didn't move.

I nudged her. I barked once again, louder this time. I waited.

But Roxy was gone.

Just like that.

I didn't understand at first. I waited all day for her to wake up. I kept looking at Mom, hoping she would do something, but Mom's eyes were full of tears. She stroked Roxy's fur one last time and whispered, "It's okay now. You can rest."

I didn't want her to rest. I wanted her to stay.

The days after that were really, really hard. I looked for Roxy in every room. I sniffed her favorite blanket. I checked under the table where she used to lie. Sometimes, I'd hear a sound and think it was her. I would stare outside the glass door for days, but it never was.

I missed her so much.

Mom and Dad missed her, too.

We were all broken, but somehow, we started to heal together.

We gave each other love every day. Cuddles, walks, quiet time. We became each other's comfort. When Mom cried, I laid my head on her lap. When I whimpered in my sleep, she whispered, "It's okay, Rosco. I'm here."

***

Later that year, we tried something new.

We went camping! I didn't know what it was, but the way Mom told me about it so excitedly, I thought it was going to be fun!

It was strange at first. There was no TV, no couch, no regular food bowls. Just trees, dirt, wind, and the sound of birds I had never heard before. And the tent! It was a funny, flappy thing that moved when the wind blew, but inside, it was warm and safe.

We slept all together in that tent. Mom, Dad, and I. I liked the way it smelled. I liked the way the stars looked outside. I felt at peace. I missed Roxy, but the place calmed me down a little. I wished she was there with us.

We went on long walks. Mom called them "hikes." I sniffed every stick, every trail, every little bug I could find. Sometimes, we'd look around for things I could chase, and they'd laugh and say, "What's Rosco hunting today?"

Mom and Dad knew I was still sad, but they were trying. So was I.

The car rides were still hard. My tummy would twist and turn, and I'd get sick sometimes. I didn't want to. I just couldn't help it. Mom always looked so sorry when it happened. She would clean me up, pet my ears, and whisper, "Poor Rosco. I know it's hard, baby."

We kept going anyway. She didn't let my car sickness stop us from having new adventures and fun.

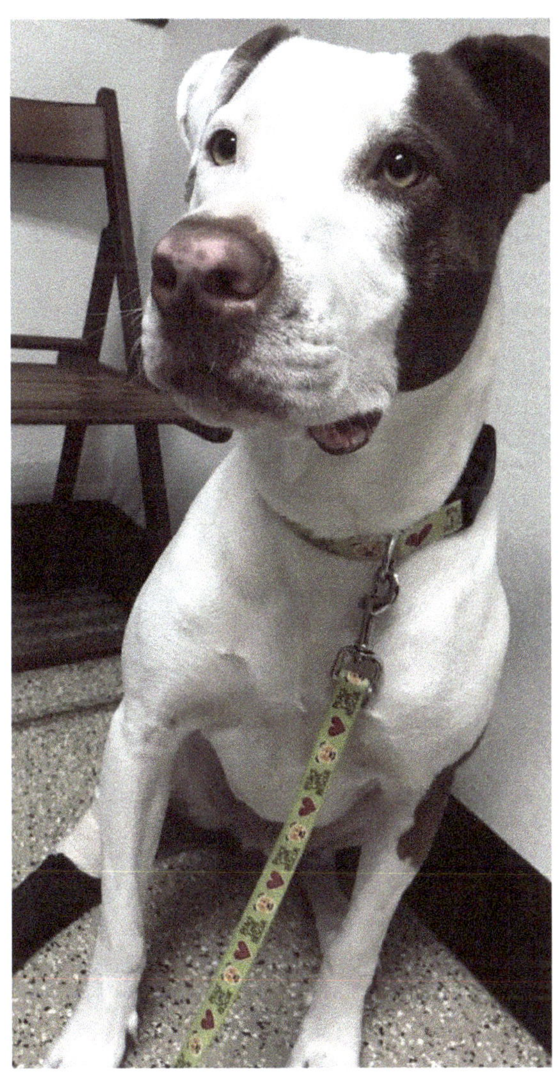

Rosco's vet visit.
He cut his right paw and had to get stitches.

Rosco was getting ready with his new sweater for camping.

CHAPTER 04 | HAPPY DAYS AHEAD

Rosco and our foster puppies.

Rosco & Milly (foster pup) 1 of 5.

Rosco's first trip to Big Sky, Montana, in the snow.

Rosco's sister, Aspen. Our rescue from Missouri.

Kaya – Rosco's sister. She was found on the street.

Rosco's cousin, Norman, who lives in New Jersey, was rescued.

Life took an exciting turn one day in 2021. I was lying comfortably on my favorite rug when I overheard Mom and Dad talking softly in the kitchen.

"What do you think about fostering some puppies?" Dad asked. "It could be good for Rosco, especially since he's been lonely after losing Roxy."

Mom sighed gently, "I think you're right. It'll keep him company. But fostering means we'll only take care of the puppies for a little while until they find their own forever homes."

Fostering? Puppies?

My ears perked up. I wasn't sure what that meant yet, but it sounded interesting. I missed Roxy terribly, and the idea of new friends made my tail wag softly.

One day, something smelled very different. It was new, sweet, and full of life. My nose twitched with excitement as I sniffed eagerly along the hallway, following the curious scent to a closed door. Behind it, tiny paws scurried, and small playful barks echoed softly. My humans called them "puppies."

I felt curious and a little unsure. My humans felt the same. I could sense it. They kept us apart at first.

"Do you think Rosco will like them?" Mom asked nervously one evening.

"He's gentle, but let's take it slow," Dad reassured her gently.

Then the day came. The doggy gate opened to the outside by mistake. We stepped carefully inside the room. Our hearts raced as five tiny fluffy puppies stopped and stared at me. Suddenly, they all rushed towards me, barking happily, their little tails wagging wildly.

"Oh my goodness! Look at Rosco!" Mom cried, smiling through tears.

"He's a natural dad!" Dad laughed.

I couldn't help myself and started wagging my tail like never before. They jumped, played, and climbed all over me, nibbling softly on my ears and paws. It felt wonderful. I barked softly, letting them know I was happy.

Every day, we played and cuddled. I showed them how to chase toys and taught them to be brave. Soon, the day came when they had to leave for their new homes in Missouri. My heart felt heavy as I watched them go. I missed their tiny paws and warm cuddles terribly. The house felt quiet again.

One day, while playing outside, a sharp pain struck my leg. I whimpered loudly.

"Rosco, are you okay?" Mom rushed over.

Dad looked worried. "We need to take him to the vet. He might have torn his ACL (Anterior Cruciate Ligament) in his knees. He'll need surgery and rest to heal properly."

They said words like "ACL" and "surgery." I didn't understand, but I knew it hurt. Mom took good care of me. Slowly, after two months, I felt better again.

That November, Mom and Dad packed us up for an eight-day road trip to Utah, Idaho, and Montana. It was my first long trip, and I did amazing, even though it was cold.

One day, we went shopping. Mom said, "Rosco needs a blanket. Let's let him pick one!"

I chose the softest, warmest one. People smiled and said how cute I was as I proudly carried it through the store. Later, I ran through soft, cold snow for the first time, barking happily with every step.

***

In October 2022, we took another road trip, this time quickly to Missouri to rescue eight puppies and bring them to hometown. The puppies were scared, just like I once was. I cuddled close, comforting them all the way home. One puppy stayed with us. It was what Mom and Dad called a doodle named Aspen, my new sister. Soon after, Kaya joined our family, too; she was rescued from the street. Now, our family had grown to three pets again. We played and barked joyfully every day.

"Rosco is so happy now," Mom said softly. "Having them here with him on our acre-and-a-half land keeps him young."

"He has his own little family again," Dad smiled warmly.

In 2023, I had another surgery. This time on my other leg. Going to the vet made me shake and whimper, but Mom's gentle words helped calm me.

"He'll be okay," Dad whispered to Mom. "We'll get through this together."

Healing took time, but I got through it because of their love.

Mom often volunteered at the pound where I was adopted. She would hug me afterward, whispering, "Rosco, there are so many dogs just like you. Every one of them deserves love, just like you."

Dad hugged Mom tight, nodding. "We're lucky to have found him."

Today, I live happily, running freely in our big yard with Aspen and Kaya. Life has taught me about friendship, bravery, and love. My humans never gave up on me, and I'll always protect them. I know I'm exactly where I'm meant to be.

PART 2:

THE REAL WORLD OF RESCUE

&

HOW I GOT STARTED

CHAPTER 05 | WHY ANIMALS NEED US – MY JOURNEY OF HELPING ANIMALS IN NEED

It all started with Rosco.

When I first saw him in that pound, timid and scared, his eyes full of questions and no way to ask them, I felt something shift inside me. He needed me, but what I didn't realize then was how much I needed him, too. Rosco changed my life completely.

After bringing Rosco home, my eyes began to open to a bigger picture. Around January 10, 2020, I was scrolling through Instagram and Facebook when I began noticing heartbreaking stories of animals all over the world. Alone, abandoned, abused. Some were starving, others injured, some chained up without shelter, waiting for someone to care. I saw puppies left in cardboard boxes, dogs trembling behind bars, and cats dumped in alleys.

I couldn't look away anymore. Rosco had made me realize that behind every sad post was a living soul who deserved love, safety, and a second chance.

Rosco is a Pitbull, a breed that has suffered so much from people's ignorance and fear. The media has painted them as aggressive, dangerous, and violent.

However, the truth is, Pitbulls are among the most loving, loyal, and affectionate dogs I've ever known. Rosco adores me unconditionally. He follows me from room to room, always wants to be near, and somehow knows when I'm having a bad day. He'll rest his head on my lap as if to say, "I'm here." His gentleness taught me just how wrong the world is about his breed.

Seeing how much love Rosco gave despite the life he had before us made me realize something: if he could still love so deeply, then maybe others could too, if only they were given the chance.

SHELTERS: The Good, The Overwhelmed, The Underfunded

I began to volunteer at the pound where Rosco had once been. The moment I walked through the gates, I was overwhelmed. Rows of kennels, filled with eyes silently begging, tails wagging cautiously, noses pressed against metal bars. Some barked for attention; others sat in silence, as if hope had long since left them. Each one of them had a story, and all of them wanted the same thing: a home.

It was then that I truly understood how many animals are thrown away like they don't matter. Many are surrendered because they got too big, or too old, or too sick. Some are left behind when people move. Others are born into lives of pain—from puppy mills, backyard breeders, or meat markets. There are dogs who have never known a soft bed or a kind hand. Cats who have never heard a gentle voice. Horses sent to slaughter. Rabbits left in cages. Every day, new lives are discarded, and shelters do everything they can, but they're overwhelmed.

People assume shelters are safe havens. The truth is, many are overcrowded and underfunded. Workers and volunteers pour their hearts into caring for the animals, but there are just too many. Some shelters don't have enough food, blankets, medicine, or even space. Sometimes they have to make heartbreaking decisions no one should ever have to make.

I couldn't sit on the sidelines anymore. I joined rescue groups across the country. I began donating, sending supplies, raising awareness, and networking with animals. I provided food, medicine, beds, toys, leashes, jackets—whatever these rescues or organizations needed. I stayed up late tagging people on posts, sharing stories, trying to find foster homes or transport help. I began helping animals not only in the U.S., but in countries like Africa, Lebanon, Brazil, the Philippines, Serbia, Venezuela, India, and so many other countries. These places don't have the resources we do. In some, dogs are tied to trees without food or water. Others are rounded up and sold for meat. It's unimaginable until you see it.

One Pitbull I helped save from a meat market in Africa still gets updates sent to me. He's healthy now, loved. He was once doomed, but someone gave him a chance. Another dog, an abandoned Pitbull in Texas, where animal neglect is heartbreakingly common, was rescued with the help of online networks. These animals are everywhere, waiting. Waiting to be seen, saved, and loved.

Through all this, I've helped several hundred animals in need, including in my own hometown.

I know it might seem like a lot of work, but trust me, you don't need to have a lot or be part of any big organization to help those in need. In fact, it can be as simple as keeping a few supplies with you, whatever you can afford, when you're out and about. I do that too. If I see a homeless person with an animal, I stop and offer food and water. I always carry supplies in my car because you never know when you'll come across a person or animal who needs help.

For me, each one of these lives mattered. Each one has a face I remember. I've seen so much: broken bones, scared eyes, mangled bodies. Sometimes it's too much. You feel like giving up, like your voice is too small, but then I look at Rosco, and I remember why I started.

The Hidden Heroism Of Adopted Pets

My other rescues mean the world to me, too. **Roxy**, our boxer, was calm and affectionate, a gentle soul who passed soon after Rosco joined us. **Kaya**, our smart and energetic terrier, was found on the streets at age two. She was the beginning of it all. Finding Kaya wandering alone, scared and unsure, was the first time I realized I couldn't turn away from an animal in need. From that moment, rescuing became a part of my life. **Aspen**, our shy little doodle, came from Missouri with eight other dogs. That was an unforgettable journey, an 18-hour drive to bring them all to safety. We rescued eight puppies, one of which we kept: Aspen. The rest found wonderful homes. Each mile of that long road trip was worth it. Their new lives began with that ride, and with love, they began to bloom. Just like children, they have their own personalities, their quirks, their stories. They make us laugh, they teach us patience, and most of all, they love without condition.

Animals, especially those rescued from trauma, need time to decompress. They don't just forget the fear overnight. You have to give them space, gentleness, and consistency. Rosco had clearly been hurt before. Loud noises scared him, sudden movements made him flinch, but over time, with love and trust, he began to feel safe again. That's the power of love. That's the gift of patience.

It's important to know: we don't save them. They save us. They teach us empathy. They teach us how to care. They teach us how to show up, again and again, even when things get hard.

I dedicate every animal I've ever helped to Rosco. He opened my eyes to the silent suffering that so many animals endure. He made me an advocate, a volunteer, a rescuer, and most of all, someone who will never stop fighting for the voiceless.

Animals are not disposable. They are not property. They are living, breathing beings with feelings, fears, and dreams. Pets are not temporary. They are forever. You don't return them because you're tired or because they're no longer convenient. You wouldn't do that to your child. Don't do it to them.

To those who fear Pitbulls: please educate yourself. They are not born aggressive. They are made that way by people who use them for fighting, abuse them, or isolate them. If you raised a Chihuahua the same way, it too would bite. Rosco is one of the kindest, most beautiful souls I've ever met. People always stop me and say, "He's so well-behaved!" They ask where I got him. I tell them proudly, "He's a rescue." And every time, I hope it plants a seed.

We need stricter laws. Harsher punishments. Greater awareness. Every act of cruelty should come with consequences. Because the pain these animals suffer isn't just physical. It's emotional. It scars them. Still, they forgive. They love again. That's the kind of heart we should all aim for.

I will continue this work for as long as I live. If I could save them all, I would. Until then, I'll be their voice. I'll be their hope. I'll fight, love, and advocate.

Every rescue animal I help, every shelter I support, every voice I raise is in Rosco's honor. I dedicate every animal saved to him, because without Rosco, I never would've known how deeply animals need us, and how deeply we need them.

"If you can't love a dog like a family member, you shouldn't get one," I often remind people.

Animals deserve our commitment. They aren't just pets; they're our teachers, companions, and best friends. Rosco taught me empathy, courage, and persistence. He made me an advocate, showing me the true meaning of unconditional love.

Thank you, Rosco. You made me who I am today. I'll be forever honored to be your mom.

Because of you!

CHAPTER 06 | THE HUMAN–ANIMAL CONNECTION

If you've ever looked into the eyes of a dog and felt like they understood you…like really *got* you…you're not imagining it.

That connection is real.

It's deep, powerful, and healing in ways that are hard to explain but easy to feel. Animals are naturally equipped with instincts that allow them to sense our emotions and respond intuitively. The bond we share with them isn't just about cuddles or going for walks. It's about love. The kind that doesn't judge, doesn't ask for anything in return.

Just shows up, day after day, heart wide open.

I'll be honest, though: that bond doesn't always click instantly. It's not always a picture-perfect story right from day one. Sometimes, it's more like a gentle dance between two nervous hearts trying to understand each other. Maybe you're carrying heartbreak or loneliness. Maybe your new companion has their own history, scars from a past you don't yet fully understand. Building trust takes patience. It takes time.

Learning to Trust Each Other

When I first brought any rescued animal home, I expected an emotional connection right away. I thought they'd know I saved them, and we'd live happily ever after.

However, it didn't work like that.

They had been hurt. I could see it in the way some of them flinched at sudden movements, or how they froze when I reached for them too quickly. They didn't understand yet that they were safe. That I wasn't going to leave or hurt them, and truthfully, I was still learning, too.

I had to be patient. I had to let go of expectations and meet them where *they* were. Some days were magical: they'd follow me from room to room, rest their head on my lap, and I'd feel like we were really connected. Other days, they'd retreat into their bed and barely look at me.

That's what trauma does: it doesn't let go all at once, but here's the thing: **the hard days are part of the bond.**

The quiet moments. The setbacks. The times when nothing seems to be working, but you show up anyway. *That* is when the real connection starts to grow.

The same goes for us humans. We might adopt an animal expecting joy, comfort, and a new best friend, and eventually, we get that. Often, though, the beginning can be a bit messy. Maybe your heart is still broken from losing a pet. Maybe you're struggling with your own grief, depression, or loneliness. Sometimes, it's hard to connect because you're just trying to survive the day.

Then one morning, you wake up and your dog is already there, sitting at your feet. Or your cat curls up next to you just when you need it most. Or your bunny hops over and nudges your hand when your chest feels heavy with anxiety. Their instincts guide them to comfort us in these vulnerable moments, sensing when we most need their quiet presence. Slowly, the bond begins. Through the quiet. Through the routines. Through the effort.

That's the beauty of the human-animal bond; it's not based on perfection. It's built on presence. On showing up, day after day, even when you're tired or heartbroken or unsure. And animals? They notice that. They feel it. They begin to trust.

Animals taught me that love doesn't always come rushing in. Sometimes, it tiptoes. It watches. It waits. When it finally arrives, it's stronger because of everything it took to get there.

How Animals Help Us Feel Better

This kind of connection isn't just emotional. It's practical, too. Animals give us a reason to get up. To keep going. They depend on us—for food, water, walks, and affection. And in giving to them, we find purpose. We find routine. We find healing. They, in return, start to bloom under our care.

Animals help us stay grounded in the present moment. When we're anxious or overwhelmed, something as simple as petting our dog or listening to our cat's purr helps calm racing thoughts and brings us back to reality. I've experienced this firsthand: after a stressful day, just sitting quietly with my animals reminds me to breathe, to slow down, to let go of worries, even if just for a few precious minutes.

I've heard so many stories from others over the years, and each one reminds me just how powerful this connection is. Like the woman who struggled with crippling anxiety and couldn't leave the house. Then she adopted a senior dog, and suddenly, she had to go outside for walks. That little bit of sunlight, that simple act of responsibility, changed her life.

Or the man who lost his wife and felt like he'd never smile again, until he started fostering kittens. He told me, "They gave me something to laugh about. They gave me a reason to talk again."

It's not always a fairytale. Some animals come with baggage. So do people. You might have to work through accidents, fear responses, separation anxiety, or even aggression. On the human side, you might feel overwhelmed, impatient, or guilty when things don't go as planned.

But through all of it—the hard days, the setbacks, the small victories—the bond grows stronger. Every time you sit quietly with your scared pup instead of getting frustrated... every time you let your rescue cat approach you on *their* terms... every time you learn to speak their language a little better, you're building something unbreakable.

Animals also help us build healthier habits. They motivate us to be more active, eat healthier, or simply get outside in fresh air more often. Walking your dog every day might seem like a small thing, but those steps add up, and before you know it, your health is improving, too. Animals don't just care for our emotional health; they help our bodies feel better as well.

This bond teaches us patience. It teaches us empathy. It teaches us to slow down and *listen*, not with our ears, but with our hearts. Animals naturally know how to read our emotions, responding instinctively when we're hurting, scared, or anxious. They sense our moods, offering gentle companionship exactly when we need it most.

There's a reason therapy animals are used in hospitals, nursing homes, and schools. Their presence lowers stress, reduces anxiety, and even helps with depression. Animals seem to have a natural radar for how we're feeling. They notice when we're sad, scared, or hurting, and they quietly move closer to comfort us. In fact, science agrees: studies show that spending time with animals helps lower stress hormones and makes our brains release chemicals that help us feel happier and calmer. Simply petting a dog or cat can lower your blood pressure, ease pain, and help with feelings of loneliness and depression.

Yes, science backs this up, but honestly, you don't need studies to prove it. Just spend time with an animal and you'll feel it—the calm, the peace, the love. They don't need to be trained therapists; their instincts naturally guide them to comfort us exactly when we need it most.

Sometimes, animals are the only ones who can reach us in our lowest moments. They don't need us to explain our feelings. They don't need us to be okay. They just stay close, offering comfort with a wag of a tail, a soft purr, or a quiet nudge.

And if you're grieving? If your heart is broken? They'll sit beside you in the dark, asking for nothing but to be near. That kind of love is not easy to find anywhere else.

So yes, animals help us, but they also *grow* with us. They heal, and they teach us how to heal, too. They forgive, and they teach us how to forgive. They love us through everything, and in doing so, they show us how to love ourselves again.

If you've ever felt like your pet "gets" you more than most people do, you're not wrong. That's the quiet beauty of this connection. It's a love that doesn't need words, just presence.

We save them, and they save us right back.

PART 3

BE THEIR VOICE:

WE NEED TO STAND UP FOR THEM

CHAPTER 07 | WHAT CAN YOU DO

You don't need to be a grown-up, a rescuer, or part of a big organization to help animals.

You just need a heart that cares.

If you've ever felt a tug in your chest when you saw a lost dog on the street, or felt angry when you heard about animals being mistreated, then guess what? That feeling inside you, that's where it starts. That's where change begins.

Helping animals isn't about doing everything. It's about doing something, and when lots of people each do something small, it adds up to something big. So whether you're a kid, a teen, or a family, here are some real ways you can make a difference, starting today.

1. Adopt or Foster

When you adopt, you're not just adding a pet to your home. You're giving someone their second chance at life.

Imagine being alone in a cold shelter, scared and unsure, with no idea what's going to happen next. Now imagine someone walks in, sees you, and says, "I choose you." That's what adoption feels like to an animal. It's a moment that changes everything.

And fostering? That's just as important. Fostering means you temporarily care for an animal until they find a forever home. It gives them space to breathe. To heal. To feel what it's like to be safe, sometimes for the very first time in their lives.

Fostering isn't always easy, especially at first. Some animals might be shy, anxious, or act out because they're scared. They might not know what toys are for or what it means to go on a walk. Some may have never seen a soft bed before, but little by little, they begin to trust. They begin to change, and you get to witness that transformation up close. You get to see their personality come to life, their tails start to wag, and their eyes begin to shine.

And yes, saying goodbye when they're adopted can hurt. It's okay to cry. It means you loved them well. Remember: because of you, they now have a future. You helped write their happy ending.

We once fostered five puppies, and Rosco stepped in like a proud parent. He licked their ears, curled up beside them, and kept watch like a guardian. We didn't know how he'd react, but he blew us away with his gentleness. That memory will stay in my heart forever. It reminded me how much animals can heal and help each other, too.

2. Donate or Volunteer

You don't have to have a lot to give a lot.

Shelters and rescues need all kinds of help, not just money. They need blankets to keep the animals warm, toys to keep them happy, leashes for walks, bowls for food, and hands to help clean and care. Even something as simple as old towels or empty water jugs can be useful.

You can hold a donation drive with your school, sports team, or neighborhood. Ask for food, supplies, or gently used pet items. You'd be amazed at how much you can collect when you invite others to join.

Volunteering is another way to help, even if you're too young to work directly with animals. Some shelters let kids come in just to sit with the animals and keep them company. You can help make posters, organize supplies, or greet visitors. Sometimes, just reading a book to a nervous dog or sitting quietly beside a shy cat can make all the difference in the world. Animals feel that presence. They feel seen, and that's powerful.

Even visiting animals, just being there, can change their day. Imagine being stuck in a cage all week and then, suddenly, someone kind walks in and sits with you. That visit becomes the highlight of the week. You matter more than you think.

And if you can foster? Do it. There are never enough foster homes. Each one saves a life. Literally.

3. Raise Awareness

There are two ways to help animals: with your hands and with your voice.

Your voice might be the most powerful tool you have.

Not everyone knows what goes on in shelters or how many animals are abandoned every day. Not everyone understands that animals feel emotions — fear, love, loneliness — just like we do. That's where you come in.

Tell their stories.

Talk about your pets and what they mean to you. Make a school project about rescue animals. Share what you've learned. Use your words to paint a picture for someone else, so they can start to care, too.

The more people know, the more they're inspired to help. Raising awareness spreads kindness like a ripple in water. It reaches places you don't even see.

Maybe your story will lead someone to adopt their next dog instead of buying one. Maybe your passion will make someone donate to a local shelter. Maybe you'll inspire a classmate to speak up for animals too.

That's how change happens.

4. Use Social Media

Social media is like a giant megaphone. When used with care, it can help rescue animals in ways we never imagined before. I've seen a single post go viral, showing a dog sitting alone on the side of the road. Within hours, people were donating, networking, and showing up to help. That's the power of sharing.

If you're online, here's how you can use your account to be a voice for the voiceless:

- Share adoptable animals and rescue stories.
- Post educational facts about pet care and responsible ownership.
- Share photos or videos of your own rescue pets and what they've taught you.
- Celebrate adoption days, fosters, and happy endings.

Always be smart. Don't post exact locations of stray animals, especially not with words like "free." There are people out there (like dog fighters) who look for those posts. Protect the animals first, always.

Instead, use your platform to educate, to uplift, to inspire. Be honest. Be kind. Be thoughtful.

Don't be afraid to be real. Share your heart. Share your journey. That's what makes people stop scrolling and really listen.

Young people are using TikTok, Instagram, YouTube, and more to spread messages of love, compassion, and advocacy. You can too.

5. Start School Clubs or Campaigns

Sometimes, the best way to create change is to gather others and light the spark together.

Starting a rescue awareness club at school might sound big, but it can begin small. All you really need is a few caring hearts and a little courage.

Begin by learning. Visit shelters. Ask questions. Learn what these animals go through. Then share what you've seen and felt. That truth will speak louder than anything.

You can plan supply drives, poster campaigns, kindness weeks, or even host guest speakers who work in rescue. Maybe create a "Rescue Pet of the Month" bulletin. Or organize a fundraiser with a local shelter.

If you're nervous or unsure, that's okay. Find a mentor. Someone already involved in the rescue can guide you. You don't have to do it alone.

Sometimes, the most powerful leaders are the quiet ones who lead with heart. If you care enough to try, you already have what it takes.

Remember: clubs and campaigns aren't about being perfect. They're about being present. About showing up. About making others care as much as you do.

6. Your Voice, Your Heart

You don't have to rescue hundreds of animals to make a difference.

You just have to love one. Help one. Speak up for one.

That one life? It matters, and the love you give them creates ripples that spread far beyond what you'll ever see.

Rescuing isn't about doing it all. It's about doing what you can, when you can, with what you have. Maybe that means offering your time. Maybe it means telling your story. Maybe it means giving someone a reason to care.

Rosco made me care. He opened my heart to a world I didn't fully see before. Every time I speak up for animals now, it's because he taught me how.

So, to every young reader out there: if you've ever wanted to help but didn't know where to start, start here. Start now. Start with kindness.

Your voice matters. Your actions matter. You matter.

Let's build a world where animals are loved, protected, and valued. Let's create a legacy filled with empathy and compassion. Let's show that even the smallest act of love can change everything, for them and for us.

CHAPTER 08 | ROSCO'S PROMISE

A Letter from Rosco to You 🐾

Hi, it's me—Rosco.

I'm lying on my soft blanket right now, the one that smells like sunshine and Mom's hugs. The window is cracked open, and I can hear the breeze ruffling the trees outside and birds singing something cheerful. Kaya is curled up beside me, and Aspen is snoring gently near the door. Everything is calm. Everything is safe.

I never used to know what that felt like.

I wanted to write you a letter. Not just to tell you about me, but to tell you what it feels like to be *one of us*. One of the dogs who had to wait behind a cage... for someone to care.

Imagine a world where dogs like me live without the promise of a home. A world where every day is filled with noise, confusion, and uncertainty. Before adoption, life was just that. A constant state of not knowing. Barking echoed through metal walls like thunder. The smell of bleach stung our noses. The floors were cold. Everything felt temporary. Nothing felt safe.

Back then, before I had a name or a home or a blanket of my own, life was very different. The world was loud. Barking echoed everywhere, like a constant storm of confusion. Doors slammed. People came and went. Some smiled. Some didn't. Every time footsteps came near my kennel, my heart jumped—not with fear exactly, but with something I didn't have a word for back then. Something like... hope.

I wagged my tail so much it hurt sometimes. Just in case today was *the* day.

But it wasn't.

Each day held a strange mix of hope and sadness. One minute, you'd think, "Maybe this is it." Next, they'd walk away, and your heart would sink again. That feeling? It carves itself into you. It makes you quiet inside.

Day after day, I waited. I stared through the bars, not understanding why no one chose me. I heard people whisper when they looked at me. I didn't know what those words meant. All I knew was that I had so much love to give, and no one to give it to.

And let me tell you… that kind of waiting? It makes you quiet inside. It makes you wonder if maybe there's something wrong with you.

Then one day, everything changed. A woman knelt down in my cage. Her eyes didn't just look *at* me. They looked *into* me. Like she could see every scared, lonely thought I was carrying. Her voice was soft. Her smile was gentle, and for the first time, I thought… maybe?

Maybe this time would be different.

And it was.

She came back. Again and again. She promised I would have a home. That I wouldn't be alone anymore. I wanted to believe her, but a part of me was still so afraid.

Being adopted into a family after months behind bars? It's confusing. It's overwhelming. I didn't know what to expect. Would they love me forever… or take me back? Would they give me the patience I needed, the love I never stopped hoping for? The questions raced through me like a storm I couldn't shake.

Rosco on a hiking trip in the mountains.

When I left the shelter with her and the man who became my dad, my paws trembled a little on the ground. I sniffed everything. The air smelled like grass and soap and something sweet. Home. That's what she called it.

But I didn't understand what *home* really meant yet.

At first, I was shy. I didn't know where to sit. I didn't know if the food was really mine. I didn't know if I was allowed to play or if I would be sent back. I didn't know how to *trust* the good things.

Sometimes I'd hide in the corner. Or watch Mom leave with my heart in my throat. I thought maybe she wouldn't come back, and when she did, I'd jump and wiggle and cry with relief, like I was telling her, "Thank you for not forgetting me."

Trying to understand a new world isn't easy for a dog who's only known loneliness. I wasn't sure how to act with my new family. I didn't know if Roxy would like me, or if I belonged at all. Every step felt like walking on eggshells. Soft, careful, uncertain.

Little by little, I started to understand.

I wasn't going to be sent away.

I wasn't just a guest.

I was family.

I began learning their rhythms.....when the house got quiet, when playtime happened, when food bowls filled, and hands reached out in love. My tail stopped hiding between my legs. My ears perked up more, and bit by bit, I showed more of who I really was. A silly, loyal, loving boy with so much heart. That's when trust began. That's when joy returned.

Mom – Should I pay the vet bill?

My paws learned the rhythm of the house, where the sunny spots were, when the food bowl clinked, how the couch cushions felt after a long nap. I learned the smell of safety. I learned the sound of laughter.

And slowly, my fear turned into something new.

Trust.

Joy.

Belonging.

Now, I have a life filled with walks and belly rubs and silly games and bedtime snuggles. I have sisters who bark with me and wrestle in the yard and curl up close when the wind howls. I have a Mom who never gave up on me, even when I chewed the couch or cried when she left. She told me, over and over, "I'll always come back, Rosco."

For two whole years, I had something called separation anxiety. Every time she left, I felt that old ache in my chest. The one that whispered, "What if she doesn't come back?" But she always did. Every single time. She was patient. She was kind. She waited for me to believe it, and slowly, I did.

And she did.

But I haven't forgotten what it felt like… to be one of the ones still waiting.

I still remember the sound of metal doors closing. I still remember the cold floor and the smell of bleach. I remember the feeling of being invisible, even while people looked straight at me.

Don't touch my ball.

Saving me from the pound was the best thing that ever happened to me. Being abandoned is the worst feeling. It breaks something inside you. But being rescued? That's what begins to heal it. That's what begins everything.

That's why I'm writing you this letter.

Because somewhere right now, another dog like me is waiting. Hiding in the back of a kennel. Watching the door. Hoping for kindness. Hoping for *you*.

The love we have to give? It's endless. Once we're safe, once we feel your arms and your voice and your patience, it comes pouring out. We become your shadows, your secret-keepers, your tail-wagging joy bringers. The bond we build with you… it's unbreakable. It's healing. Not just for us, but for you, too. Because adopting us doesn't just change our lives. It changes yours.

Rescue stories like mine? They're full of transformation. They're filled with second chances, redemption, and the kind of loyalty that makes every bad day better.

Please, if you can, adopt.

Don't shop for dogs like toys on a shelf.

We aren't things. We're hearts with fur and tails.

We feel everything.

And when we're given a second chance, we don't forget. We don't waste it. We love harder than you ever thought possible.

If you've already adopted someone like me, thank you. From the bottom of my big dog heart, thank you.

And if you haven't yet, but you're thinking about it… just know this:

Striking a pose.

We don't need perfect homes. We just need *your* home.

We don't expect you to have all the answers. Just bring your patience, your kindness, and your promise to try.

We'll do the rest.

We'll love you forever.

We'll be your shadow, your warmth, your joy.

I'm Rosco. I was rescued.

But really… love rescued me.

And I love my mommy so much. I can't thank her enough for the way she gave me her heart, and still does, every single day. She's not just my human. She's my best friend.

And now, I want to help rescue others….with my story, with this letter, with *you*.

Thank you for listening. Thank you for caring.

And thank you for being a voice for the ones still waiting.

With a full heart and a wagging tail,

Rosco

My favorite toy from my Auntie Christine.

PART 4

ROSCO'S WORLD:

A HEARTFELT ADVENTURE (FICTION)

CHAPTER 09 | ROSCO & THE PACK

Rosco's POV

They say that after everything we go through—every storm, every scar, every moment the world feels too loud or too lonely—there's a place where we find peace.

But let me say it how I really feel it.

After all the hard stuff... after the days that felt too long and the nights that felt too cold... there's a place where things finally settle. Where the barking doesn't bounce off cold walls. Where the floor isn't hard and shiny and scary. Where hope doesn't walk past your cage without looking in.

For me and the others, that place is real. We call it **The Haven**.

I don't know how we ended up here exactly. Maybe we dreamed it into being. Or maybe love created it once we were finally safe. All I know is that one day I opened my eyes, and the world around me wasn't the same anymore. The ground felt soft, not sharp. The air smelled like pine trees and fresh rain instead of bleach and sadness. The sun didn't just shine, it wrapped around me like a warm hug that said, *You made it.*

And the best part? I wasn't alone.

I never thought I'd see Roxy again. But there she was.

She stood at the top of the hill, her tail swaying gently, ears perked with that calm curiosity she always had. She wasn't barking or pacing or anxious. She was just there... still and waiting. Just like she always used to. Quiet, loyal, steady.

My heart jumped, and I ran to her. No hesitation. As soon as I reached her, I pressed my nose into her fur, and the second I felt her warmth… strong, familiar, grounding… I knew I was home. Again.

She didn't have to say a word. Roxy never needed to. I had so many feelings in that moment. Shock, happiness, even a little disbelief. However, the second I looked into her eyes, all those emotions turned into one single truth.

We were together again.

And we weren't the only ones.

All around us were dogs. Dozens, maybe more. Some we knew, some we didn't, but we could tell, just from the way they walked, that every one of them had a story. You could see it in their eyes, the way they moved. Some stepped slowly, carefully, like they were still learning to trust the ground under their paws. Others ran wild and free, full of joy, like they'd been waiting for this place forever and were finally letting themselves feel it.

Aspen was there, of course. My soft, quiet sister with the dreamy eyes. She's never been one to bark a lot. She listens more than she speaks. Back in the real world, she used to stay close to the walls when people came near. But here? Here she runs through the grass with her ears flying and her tail high, like she finally figured out what freedom feels like. She found her bravery in The Haven.

Then there's Kaya. Wild, fast, brilliant Kaya. Her body moves like a rhythm all its own, quick and full of purpose. She's always the first one to charge after a squirrel-shaped shadow and the last one to come back. In The Haven, she doesn't hold back. She sprints across meadows, dives into piles of leaves, and starts games like a whirlwind of joy. She even organizes races and digging contests under the old tree stumps. We call her the ringleader, and honestly, she loves that title.

And then there's Blue.

Oh, Blue.

He's built like a baby horse with legs that don't always cooperate and a bark that could shake the sky. But Blue? He's all heart. He flinches when voices get too loud, and he's terrified of thunder, but in The Haven, he curls up in the sunlight with his favorite stuffed duck clutched tight between his paws. When we nap together, he snores so loud that butterflies get knocked off course mid-flight. We wouldn't have it any other way.

Now Pixie... Pixie is a whole situation by herself. She's tiny, maybe the size of a loaf of bread, but you'd think she ran the entire pack. Actually, I think she *does*. One bark from her and we all listen. I once saw Blue hand over a stick like it was royalty passing down a crown, all because Pixie gave him that look. She's sassy and sharp, but if she sees you feeling low, she'll curl up right by your face and hum a soft little growl that somehow makes your chest feel lighter.

Then there's Tank, our naptime captain. Big bulldog. Droopy eyes. Slow steps. Softest heart. He finds the best sun patches and shares them with anyone who needs them. When your thoughts get heavy or your heart feels tight, Tank is the one who will lean in close, rest his chin on your shoulder, and just *be there* without saying a thing. He gets it. We all do.

Every one of us came from something hard. Things we didn't choose. Abandonment. Fear. Hurt. We carry those pieces with us, tucked deep where no one can see them. But here in The Haven, those pieces start to fit together into something else. Something softer.

We've learned that healing shows up in strange ways. Like the squish of mud between your paws. Or a stick you don't want to share. Or running through tall grass without a leash, just for the joy of it. Every evening, when the sky turns lavender and the stars flicker on one by one, we all gather on the hilltop. We lie close. Bodies pressed together. Tails brushing, ears twitching. Roxy always lies beside me, one paw resting gently over mine like a promise.

Sometimes we hear the wind bring whispers from the old world. Familiar voices. Names being called in sleep. Humans we loved, still dreaming of us. We remember. Oh, we remember, and when we do, we lift our heads and send our love back with a quiet howl. The kind that only hearts can understand.

But even with all the peace we've found, there's something we never forget.

The ones still waiting.

The dogs curled up on cold floors behind bars. The puppies shivering in cardboard boxes. The cats hiding under porches, hoping someone sees them. We dream of them. We feel their longing in our bones.

So every night, we howl. Not because we're sad, but because we're promising.

"We see you. We remember. And one day, you'll be here too."

Because in The Haven, nobody is forgotten.

Nobody is unloved.

And nobody ever has to be alone again.

CHAPTER 10 | THE BIG ESCAPE

Rosco's POV

It was a quiet evening in The Haven. The stars were blinking softly above us, and our pack was curled up together in the tall grass, bellies full and hearts calm. The air smelled like lavender and fresh earth, and for a little while, everything felt perfectly still.

But then, something stirred in my chest. A feeling I couldn't shake. I lifted my head and looked out across the open fields. Roxy stirred beside me, her wise eyes already locked on the horizon. She felt it too. Aspen sat up slowly, ears flicking toward the distant hills. Kaya, who'd been wiggling in her sleep, blinked toward the woods like she was already on alert. Even Blue, who usually snores like an old bear, let out a deep breath and rolled to his feet.

This wasn't just a feeling anymore.

It was a call.

Somewhere beyond our peaceful world, there were animals still waiting. Still scared. Still wondering if love would ever find them the way it found us. The Haven was wonderful, no doubt about it, but it wasn't complete. Not while so many others were still stuck in places filled with fear and silence.

So that night, we made a decision. All of us. No barking, planning, or debate. Just a quiet, shared understanding.

We were going back.

Not to stay, and not to relive all the hard memories, but to help. To search. To rescue. We wanted to be the ones who showed up when no one else did. The ones who opened the cage. The ones who knew, deep down, that every animal deserved a second chance.

We weren't leaving The Haven because we didn't love it. We were leaving because we loved it so much, we had to share it.

Just before sunrise, we met beneath the Dream Tree. It's an old willow with long, glowing leaves that shimmer like they've been kissed by morning dew. Some say it only opens its door when your heart is ready. I wasn't sure if that was true or not, but as we stood under its branches, something amazing happened. The tree leaned just slightly, and right in its center, a hollow opened up wide enough for a dog to walk through.

Kaya was the first to step forward, tail high and fearless. "Let's go make some noise," she said with a playful grin.

Aspen followed quietly, brave in her own soft way, her eyes steady and thoughtful.

Then came Blue, holding his little stuffed duck like it was a mission badge.

Pixie climbed onto my back and settled in like a queen on her throne. She claimed her legs were too tiny for long-distance travel, but we all knew she just liked riding in style.

And Roxy... Roxy walked beside me, shoulder to shoulder. She didn't speak. She didn't have to. Her steady presence said it all: this was the right thing to do.

As I stepped through the opening in the tree, the world around us began to shift. The light dimmed. The air turned cooler, and in just a few steps, we found ourselves in a place that made my heart tighten.

We were back in a shelter. Or something like it.

The ground was hard again. The air smelled sharp and sterile, like bleach and sadness. Barking echoed everywhere. Fast, loud, desperate.

But we weren't here to stay.

We were here to free.

We moved through the corridors quietly, like shadows on a mission. Kaya found the first cage, where a young beagle crouched in the corner, trembling, eyes wide with fear.

"Hey, little one," she said gently, tail wagging low. "You ready to leave this place?"

The beagle whimpered.

Blue walked over and laid down right outside the bars, blocking the cold draft with his big warm body.

Aspen stepped forward and nosed the latch. We're not sure how, but it clicked open just like that. The door creaked, and the little beagle stepped out slowly. He looked at all of us like he couldn't believe it was real. I knew exactly what that felt like.

"You're safe now," I told him, my voice calm and steady. "Come on. You can walk with us."

And we kept going, one kennel at a time. We found a mother cat curled around her tiny kittens. An old lab with cloudy eyes who hadn't lifted his head in days. A group of rabbits in a wire cage, dirty and wide-eyed but still curious.

Wherever we went, we opened doors.

But not just with paws or noses.

We opened them with presence.

With the way we approached gently, never rushing. With the way we waited patiently, giving them time. With the quiet understanding that comes from having once been forgotten, and the promise that they wouldn't be forgotten again.

Some animals didn't come out right away. That was okay. We left scent trails behind……little markers of safety and comfort, like breadcrumbs leading to something better. A soft pawprint here. A curl of fur there. Whispers of The Haven left behind in case they wanted to follow later.

At the far end of the building, we found a door that led outside. The air smelled like pavement and far-off cars, but beneath all that, we could feel it… that familiar tug pulling us home. The Haven was calling us back.

"Ready?" Kaya asked, her tail swishing, her eyes full of spark and purpose.

One by one, we stepped out into the light.

And something incredible happened.

The ground beneath our paws softened.

The sky opened wide and poured in golden light.

And behind us, the animals who had followed, along with the ones who had only dared to hope, found the path open too.

It wasn't fairy tale magic with wands and sparkles. It was something better.

It was love, turned into action.

It was every human who had ever knelt down in front of a cage and whispered, "I see you. I choose you."

It was every rescue and foster who gave their time and their heart. Every voice that said, "You matter. You're not invisible."

And us? We were just the messengers.

The pack.

The ones who had once waited and wondered… and now came back to say, "No more waiting."

We led them home.

Not just to food bowls and soft beds and collars with names— though many would find those too.

We led them to safety.

To freedom.

To hope.

And maybe, if the world was feeling especially kind, to someone on the other side of the Dream Tree. Someone with arms open, whispering, "There you are. I've been waiting for you."

Because every rescue starts with a moment like that.

And while it might feel like magic, it's really just love.

Showing up.

Again. And again. And again.

Thank you for reading my mommy's book!